Journeys
through
Creative Eyes

FIRST EDITION

©opyright 2015 by Gary Drury Publishing™

ISBN-10: 0692599800
ISBN-13: 978-0692599808 (Drury's Publishing)

DrurysPublishing.com

Kentucky

Produced in The United States of America.

Contents

Poems

YOUR TIME (LUKE 16: 19 TO 31)

The master of all time has permitted you to view
what your allotted time to live will realize for you
the 16th chapter of Luke tells the story of two men who
lived lives as different on this earth,
as two men could ever do.

They both found out that when they died
life continued as before
but in another dimension, for time
is not measured anymore,
Lazarus was now in paradise and he was satisfied
the rich man was in torment, and in his pain he cried
for just one drop of water, it is now his great request
in fear, regret and anguish, he did beat upon his breast.

But he was told there was no way, nothing anyone could do
the great gulf fixed between them, no one could travel through
not enough regret to change it, to repent no good will do
no gold or silver, prayer of saint, will alter this for you,

"Oh please, if you can't help me, then perhaps
you'd be so kind
to send someone to those I love, the ones I left behind
for they must choose to not come here,
and choose while they still can
for time will cease to be for them, like it will for every man."

In your lifetime all of you, have heard that He would come
the worthy one to answer to, the work that needed done
to make sure hell would be occupied,
by those it was intended for
the time to choose is now, before your time will be no more.

— © Janet Goven

SILENT NIGHT

Silent Night, Holy Night
the stars were never shining
quite this bright,
for this night is special
a message it brings
as the whole world lay sleeping
a host of angels sings.
Silent Night, Holy Night
brings God's answer
to our direst plight,
for we in sin and darkness lay
while our savior lies
in His manger hay
a baby born, to live, then die
for the sins of man, they crucify
the one who is the reason
for this
Silent Night, Holy Night
now we must follow
in His eternal light
for Jesus Christ is the only way
the Light of the World
we must bid Him stay
until He brings us to
our final
Silent Night.........

— © Janet Goven

SOLOMON . . . SELF-INDUCED BONDAGE

Solomon, Solomon, in all of his glory
such wisdom and fame did this one man achieve
but when we get to the end of this wonderful story
ultimately he did cause God's heart to grieve.
For he led himself into self-induced bondage
lust for women of great beauty, he had not a few
could no longer distinguish what was sin in God's eye
waning wisdom and power to know what to do.

Tenderhearted with love for the God of his father
this youth in humility, cried for wisdom to please
this God who had chosen him king over His people
in worship and gratitude, he fell to his knees.
God honored his desire, granted wisdom and more
gave him riches beyond measure and peace in the land
his wisdom spread abroad, all the earth knew his name
this Solomon who God upheld, with His mighty right hand.

Then somewhere in his lifetime, we don't know just when
the lust of his eyes and his flesh rose above
his fear of his God in whose ways he had walked
now women and little gods did receive all his love.
We wonder, do we not, how a man of such stature
could depart from the ways of the God of his youth
who had given him life, in all of it's splendor
in his abundance he lost sight of this ultimate truth.

That God's word is forever, His ways they change not
He is holy and righteous His promise to keep
to those who are His, who have vowed never to pay
for the sins that the season of pleasure would reap.
For we all have a Solomon living within, let us
covet instead things that would help us break through
win the battle still raging, and with confidence declare
to the God of our fathers, we had always stayed true.

— © Janet Goven

ESCAPE WITH ME

Can you count the snow/lakes
catch a ray of sun
can you follow the rainbow
to find where it's begun?
Can you turn on the silvery moon
ride upon a star
seize a bolt of lightning
to bring it where you are?
Paint color on the whitest cloud
silence the thunder roar
can you run through the raindrops
from angry sky's downpour?
Just imagine if you can
this fantasy with me
escaping earthbound gravity
for a playground in the galaxy!

— © Janet Goven

BEAUTIFUL SKY

Holiday fireworks light up the ebony
Sky, adding adornments to the heavens
Along with booming noises from bright rockets
Augment sound and music to the celebration
The chorus of stars, are sensitive to
An interruption of tranquility
Festivities offer fun to some
Those residing with a higher being
Do their best to accept

— © **Sandra Glassman**

ALCOVE SPRING SPIRITS

thick green grass

nodding daffodils
plump red
tulips

the scent of
wild plum blossoms
drifting on warmed wind

walnut trees
popping fuzzy buds

cold water
gushing up out
of lime stoned depths

full of
Carved

names
going
west

in The Gold Rush

— © Sheryl L. Nelms

SOUTH DAKOTA SAILORS

lounging in deck chairs
on bluegrass lawns
outside summer cabins
rimming Lake Poinsett

they talk jibs
and riggings
and catamarans

and watch
sailboats
fly

back and forth
across wrinkled water

sailors trapped
in those prairie potholes

like mosquito larva
caught in

a drying puddle

— © Sheryl L. Nelms

MONTANA WIND

it rushes up
through dry feather grass
pushes the antelope
over the ridge

drops off
a limestone cliff

rolls along the slope
through the scrub cedar

rattles the branches
shakes a nesting
turtle dove
into flight

riffles out across the Rosebud River

catches in thick thorns
of a plum thicket
rimming the bank

and lays down
dying

moaning its wau ya pi song

— © **Sheryl L. Nelms**

THE ROAD TO NOWHERE

There's a road that goes to nowhere,
Past the peaks of discontent
And those who make the journey
Have neither gained nor spent.

It exists not on a map,
But no one seems to care;
There is no cause for haste
On the trek from here to there.

Some roads lead to glory,
Others garner fame,
But this is one, when once begun —
You have only yourself to blame.

So if you're prone to wanderlust,
Upon the wayward track,
Be prepared to face the woes
Of never turning back.

— © C. David Hay

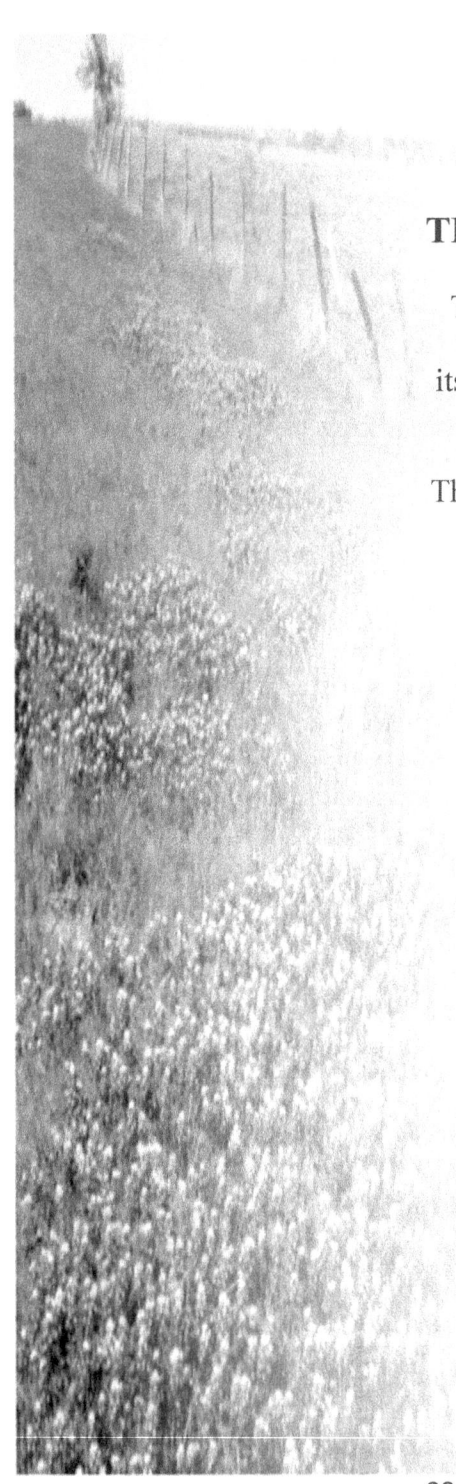

THE GARDEN'S BEAUTY

The verdant garden quietly waits
for all the world to see,
its beautiful paths of brilliant gold
that glow with majesty.

The trees of green reach to the sun
and sing a song of glee
rustling on the gentle breeze
as soft as it can be.

Flowers wear their pastel gowns
of white and pink and blue
bordering on the golden paths
awash with crystal dew.

This is a place of joy and love
that shares its calming peace,
a place to find serenity
where all our problems cease.

The garden has a magic
that warms our heart and soul,
a place to find contentment
where we can all feel whole.

— © **Sheila B. Roark**

SPIRIT

I am the spirit of nature
residing in all living things,
from the trees that stand tall in the forest
to the Cardinals with bright crimson wings.

I give the leaves subtle music
as they rustle way up in the trees,
and paint all the flowers with colors
inviting the birds and the bees.

Babbling brooks sing out loudly
under a bright golden sun,
while squirrels bury nuts in the soil
then play til the day's finally done.

I am the spirit of nature,
a gift from Our Father above,
a way to show all of His people,
that His gift comes from deeply felt love.

— © **Sheila B. Roark**

RUSTIC AUTUMN

The world is dressed in rustic hues
adorned in reds and browns,
where orange pumpkins can be see
upon the ecru grounds.

Autumn has arrived once more
along with cooling air
while leaves prepare to leave the trees
as quiet as a prayer.

It is a muted time of year,
when winter's on its way,
a time to dream of springtime warmth
that seems so far away.

The rustic gown that nature wears
is painted with great care,
a gift of beauty and delight
that all the world can share.

— © **Sheila B. Roark**

24

SHADOWS AND STONES

The shadows and the stones, I find,
Are all that life has left behind
Of what was once, a castle grand,
That overlooked pastoral land.
And as I look, I seem to see
The way this mansion used to be.
From every turret, pennants flew,
Against a sky so deeply blue.
From every window pane, the light
Reflected from the sun.
At night, The candles beckoned any eye,
From carriages a-passing by.
People's voices, laughter, song,
Filled the air the whole day long.
There must have been a lady, fair,
Who welcomed all who traveled there.
And too, a handsome lord, to ride
Across the wooded countryside.
Now, no one even can recall
Who held this keep; who made it fall.
But buried deep, lie ancient bones,
Beneath the shadows and the stones.

— © **Betty L. Hebert**

SOME ICE NEVER THAWS

Autumn leaves wither and die
as blue turns to dark gray sky,
yes green grass can turn to brown
and like a thief that flees
a town winter's flakes
come tumbling down.
Which is worse, forgotten verse
of a song that once was lover's
woo, or a valentine that once
was red but changed to
broken hearted blue!?
We all shed tears for departed ones
be they gone for short or long
our souls can die in a gilded cage
when we have nowhere else
to belong.
April showers can grow sweet
flowers for hours of fragrant
scent, but loneliness can bring
a vulture that cannot sing
a lullaby heaven meant.
Demon fangs and demon claws
can shred the cause of love's
sweet pause, the summer sun
may warm the soul but
some ice never thaws!

— © Gerald Heyder

WHAT DID YA DO NEW YEAR'S?

My personality wasn't ready for surrender
Too much ego- maybe
Knuckleheads were getting on my nerves.
Too much pride masking a nugget of self pity.
Hate players, hate players hating, hate the hating.
Looking for a warmth,
the kind that calms and gives me a sense of
detachment from society's harsh ways.
Hardened by hardships.
Dismayed by results.
I still check for inner peace.
I need its enormous strength and balance.
While I get it out of hibernation,
I'll take the raw emotion off my shoulder.
My inner peace will arrive without fanfare.
It will simply be there.

— © **Milton Kerr**

TEA TIME

The playhouse stood beside the bed
Where scarlet poppies raised their head.
With columbines, carnations too.
The lily-of-the-valley grew
Beside the door in early spring
And was there ever anything
That smelled so good? I used to play
Out in my small house every day
And I'd pretend that I was grown,
With children of my very own.
On down the yard, there was a gate
That led into a field. I'd wait
And watch as suppertime drew near
To see my father first appear.
Around the comer, by a mill
Where people buy their flour still
And when he came, he'd stop awhile
Inside my playhouse. With a smile,
He'd sip a cup of make-believe tea
And spend a little time with me.

— © Betty Lou Hebert

WEDNESDAY'S CHILD

There is a childhood verse I know,
Perhaps you know it too.
"Wednesday's child is full of woe"
For me, it's really true.
My father died when I was young.
I hardly can recall.
When a siren song was sung,
My mother left us all.
Me, a brother and my aunt
And though we muddled through,
My aunt soon left us and much worse,
My brother left me too!
I went into a cabaret
To dance and sing each night
Though I smiled and laughed I knew,
That this life wasn't right
And so I packed my bag and left
Upon a west-bound stage.
When I reached San Francisco
I knew I'd turned a page!
I got work in a hat shop,
Where I helped create chapeaus.
So now I am a lady
And I have attentive beaus!
Where my life is headed though
I cannot begin to know,

— © Betty Lou Hebert

THE LAST DANCE

Alzheimer's
has made
her

forget
to brush
her teeth

take a bath

what words
to say

and food
to eat

too shaky to stand alone
or sit in a chair

she still
loves

to cuddle
in her husband's arms

and waltz

— © Sheryl L. Nelms

PARKINSON'S

No definite
Test
For it

the neurologist
says
just walk
the straight
line

answer
the nurse's
questions

Who is the president
what country
are we in

remember
apple
table
penny

spell world
backwards
and meet
dementia
head
on

— © Sheryl L. Nelms

30

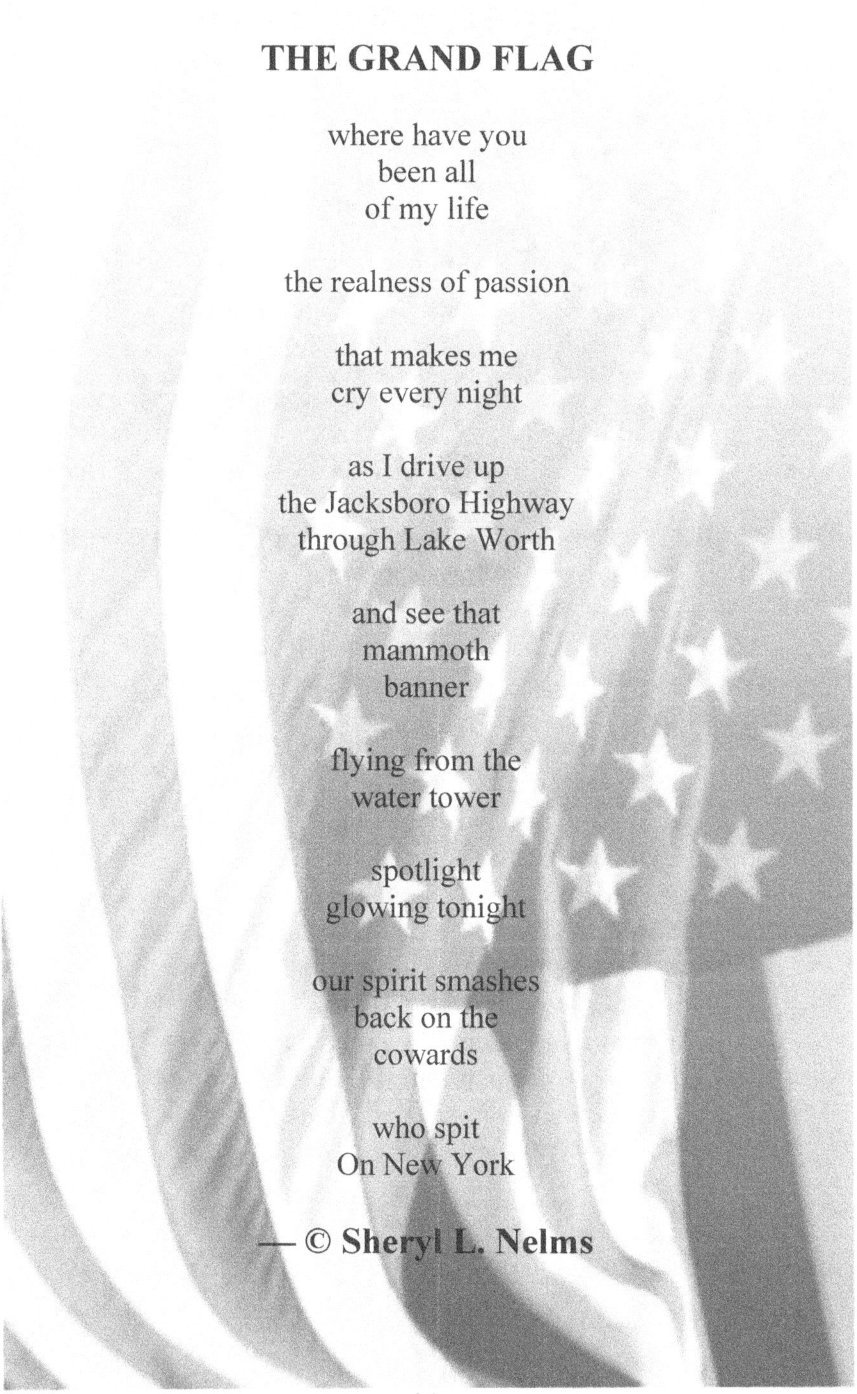

THE GRAND FLAG

where have you
been all
of my life

the realness of passion

that makes me
cry every night

as I drive up
the Jacksboro Highway
through Lake Worth

and see that
mammoth
banner

flying from the
water tower

spotlight
glowing tonight

our spirit smashes
back on the
cowards

who spit
On New York

— © Sheryl L. Nelms

PENNY FOR THOUGHTS

Where are You, when the plane was blown
Out of the beautiful blue sky
Where are YOU, hearing about innocent people
Whose blood is being the decor of the streets
Where are you when a young policeman was
The target for a deranged killer without mercy
Perhaps I should ask" Where is your voice"
I know silence is not heard, outrage is loud
The scope of humanity, such as it is must
React, why it refuses remains a mystery

— © Sandra Glassman

EMPTY HOURS

For countless hours every day
he occupies the wooden rocker
rhythmically swaying back and forth
oblivious to the world around him.

His old and faded eyes
stare out blankly seeing nothing,
not realizing the beauty he is missing
since the interloper invaded his brain.

Once he was a dynamo accomplishing so much,
but that was before the merciless attack
that has left him a limp and empty shell
unaware of what he's lost.

When his wife looks at him
her heart breaks into little pieces
bringing on flowing tears
as she mourns the loss of her lover and friend.

He feels uncomfortable around her for
he has no idea who she is,
and doesn't understand why
she keeps telling him she loves him.

The only thing that comforts him
is his rocking chair,
and so he rocks back and forth for hours
unaware of the world that passes him by.

— © Sheila B. Roark

AUTUMN IN ITS GLORY

The walkway to the little house
is lined with gold and brown,
along with orange and some red
from leaves now floating down.

And as the breeze this autumn day
gently blows the leaves,
a rhythmic dance is seen by all
that only nature weaves.

In this time of cooling air
the leaves bid trees goodbye,
and squirrels dig up their hidden nuts
under a clear fall sky.

The glory of these autumn days
is plainly seen by all
as leaves dance softly on the breeze
while answering nature's call.

— © **Sheila B. Roark**

Stories

HAVE YOU SEEN THEM?

by Janet Goven

I've been wondering lately what has happened to a few words I don't hear much anymore. Words of timeless truth and worth that sustained the foundation of this country. You know, when people really were like minded and everyone understood. When culture meant all of us, our citizenship together; and most often we really were the United States.

So, let me ask you, what is proper today? What is the right thing to do? And how about respect? Is everyone deserving of it?

Does anyone get it? Our parents, our elders, those in authority over us, who have the knowledge, wisdom, goodness and compassion, that work hard for our ultimate good. Do we respect them anymore?

How about moderation? It means just enough and no more. No excess in eating, drinking, or, whatever you love to do. It means self-control. You cared enough about your "self" to keep control. There was an unspoken knowledge of truth inside of us that told us too much is not good for us. Do you remember restraint? Now it is over indulgence in everything.

Modesty is sadly missing also. You know, when more was covered than was showing. When it was not proper to seduce or tease in the way we dressed or behaved ourselves. Ah...there's a word we don't use much anymore. Behave.

Why are these words and what they mean missing here today? Eroded away, little by little, until that still small voice we used to call our conscience, doesn't speak to us anymore. Have we silenced it through constant suppression, becoming like zombies who have no character? Does character matter? Someone you can trust?

Integrity says it all. When we always behave the right way whether anyone is watching or not. Being what we say we are, all the time. A person who has a conscience that is still alive.

Where is truth? When you throw out truth, justice goes with it. No boundaries, no restraints, how do you pass judgment with no absolute guidelines?

These words are moral fibers we must weave into the fabric of our society. Without the timeless worth of these words, which is what makes us who we are and what we are, we will not be able to continue to be the formidable force for good in this world.

We have lived and watched this time come upon us. We are living a dying way of life. What we must do is pray, then stand for truth whenever we hear it, live a modest life in moderation, exercise self control, always do the right thing, and believe that God knows if and when the strength of these timeless truths, will once again be the way of these United States.

THERE IS NO REASON TO VOTE UNLESS YOU CAN RESOLVE YOU'RE DIFFERENCES

by Juliet Rhodes Lynch

I say potatoes and you say patatoes or tamatoes and you say tomatoes. Does it really matter how it is pronounced? Not really! But, people will argue over this when ever it comes up in their conversations with others. The same goes for just about anything you want to talk about. I have lived in this community and worked in this community for 38 years. What are the things that people like most of all that live here or in the area? I know one thing that people spend time doing is [jawing}, talking, arguing, and lying. Yes, I said lying! People don't seem to realize they are lying, or arguing. The brightest star in the war on being a better community and moving forward is not listening to all the gossip and trash talk about your people who run for office. Get to know them in the community and as your neighbor, and most of all what they do all the time for the community and people and churches. If it is not what you want for the people who make decisions for that office and the community, Then you should not VOTE for them. If you don't make a point to pay attention to your surroundings and the people and what they do with their lives, then you can not VOTE WITH A CLEAR VIEW . YOU ARE VOTING for nota, zilch, a big fat zero. You can people watch and they won't know your watching them .If you take some time to sit in places where you know that they spend time ...ball fields, churches, offices, out to eat, walking on the street, sitting on benches in town ...with their families, camping, many inside activities, and outside activities. WATCH, LISTEN, AND MAKE NOTES IN YOUR MIND OF WHAT YOU SEE AND HEAR ...AND THE ACTIONS THAT THEY PRESENT IN PUBLIC, IN THEIR FRONT YARD, OR WHERE EVER YOU SEE THEM ...CATCHING THEM OFF GUARD IS WHAT YOU WILL FACE ...DURING THE ELECTION, AFTER THE ELECTION ....AND FOR THE TIME THEY ARE IN OFFICE. If you pick and choose wisely you will be rewarded with wise intelligent people , who will work to better the community and use the correct resources to make the community a place to live and be proud of. IF, you can't realize that it is time to make correct choices and not just walk into the voting place and just pick randomly, because you've heard the name, or just to be voting ...You must give your true wisdom and power to vote wisely and know the people who your going to vote for. If you are a praying person, or a praying family, you should consider praying about these people who are running and pray about who you should vote for. The Lord will give you impression to your mind if you ask Him to show you who is the best person for the job. What you do is up to you, but if you do it wrong, you have no one to blame but yourselves. When your town and community turn into something that is an embarrassment, and goes to HECK in a hand basket, you can smile and cheer and say I help do that. Laugh not, but if you choose right, and the community starts a brand new journey at being a delightful, Inspiring, and growing, maturing community. CHOOSE AS YOU WILL, BUT, LISTEN TO TO AN INNER VOICE THAT WILL DIRECT YOU AND GIVE YOU AND THE COMMUNITY A NEW BEGINNING.

BROOKLYN FROLICS

by Susan C. Barto

Susan loved the sidewalks of New York. Brooklyn seemed the most perfect of all worlds to live in. She and her cousins reigned over the neighborhood—their throne being the old green bench in front of the two family house. She and her brother bill lived in the two family house with her cousins Andy, Claire and Merry. Another cousin Christine came to visit each weekend. Each day the neighborhood children gathered at the old green bench and played time, truth or consequences, and hide and seek. They listened for the ding of the good humor truck as good Uncle Joe bought ice cream for the whole neighborhood and kept mum so that they could indulge in another treat in the evening ALTHO they were only allowed good humor once a day.

Susan's closest friend of her heart was Bubbles, the daughter of a Rabbi who lived next door. Together they walked their doll carriages through the neighborhood and called each other sister. Susan had no other sister, but Bubbles and her cousins seemed as close to sisters as anyone could wish for. Real life began and ended on the streets of Brooklyn together with the neighborhood cronies. Years

41

later when she read the peanuts cartoons, Susan was reminded of this. The screech sound that issued forth from adult mouths Susan agreed with. The only voices worth listening to were the voices of siblings and friends. Like Charles Schultz, Susan and her friends thought of adults as only shrill voices issuing from tall giants whose only purpose seemed to be to annoy and get in the way of the children's fun.

Susan's favorite excursion consisted of a trip to the library that included crossing the wide traffic filled ocean parkway with its bicycle paths and walking paths where young mamas pushed their opulent baby carriages. After crossing ocean parkway that some-times was strewn with horse chestnuts from the horseback riding crowd, she passed the chicken slaughter house with her eyes averted and passed the dry cleaners where Hitler hung in effigy. After passing these sights the library came into view, and for an hour or so Susan lost herself in the sights and smells of the library-the smell of the books and the library paste, the look of the stacks and rows of books stacked so neatly on the shelves. She chose her newest Mary POPPINS or Betsy, TACY, and TIBB, and cradled the books in her arms as she wended her way back home to the stoop and the old green bench. She could not read on the bench, however, too many distractions from the other children. She read on her bed at night. Her home was filled with turbulent arguments between her parents, and the books served to drown out the reality and transport her to other worlds. Something reading managed to do for Susan for the rest of her life.

Susan's father surprised her with a dollhouse big enough to enter and equip with her dolls and doll carriages and doll furniture. She and Bubbles filled with glee put their dolls and things in the doll-house and went to the store to buy crepe paper to make curtains for the dollhouse. When they returned she discovered that Billy had converted the dollhouse into a clubhouse and a clubhouse unfortu-nately, for Susan , it remained. However, as a clubhouse it was enjoyed by the entire neighborhood and on it they climbed via the lilac bush to the roof of the clubhouse and from there to the roofs of the neighborhood garages. They could leap from one roof to anoth-er—kings of the world and the neighborhood they believed themselves to be and indeed until they were called in for lunch or dinner they were.

School proved to be a pleasant addition to neighborhood life. The grade school—P.S. 215—around the corner from their house and next to a candy store-seemed like one more adventure in Susan's life to be savored and enjoyed. She could already read, and she promptly skipped the first grade going from kindergarten to second grade in one leap. On the way home the children stopped in at the candy store where they bought school supplies and had their choice of penny candy arranged in a colorful array. The hard part to Susan,choosing which candies on which to spend her pennies, engaged her each afternoon. Homework proved to be easy or non existent, and life on the street engaged the children. Stoop ball, stick ball, bouncing the spalding pink balls and turning their knees over the ball used countless hours. Bouncing the ball to the tune of sidewalks of New York, Susan loved this life.

When the time came for her to learn to roller skate, Andy grabbed her one morning when she came onto the street and put the skates on her feet. "Today, Susan, you learn to roller skate." Since Andy was boss, Susan skated. Riding the two wheeler proved to be the same formula. No one ever heard of training wheels. Andy said, "today you ride the two wheeler/ and Susan rode. She fell off into a bramble bush at the end of the street, got back on the bike scratched and a bit bloody, but brave enough to ride back home on the two wheeler. 'BRAVO', Andy cried.

Life tumbled on in this agreeable fashion on the streets of Brooklyn until Susan hit eight years old. At that time her father moved her family to a gorgeous house on a tree lined street in the suburb of summit, new jersey. Susan experienced a trauma from which she never completely recovered. Forever, her heart would beat faster when she arrived in the city. However, she relished visits to and from Brooklyn, and the Brooklyn frolics she had experienced in her first eight years remained with her always. East side, west side all around the town. The tots played ring around rosy London bridge is falling down. Boys and girls together. Me and MAMIE

O'ROURKE. We tripped the life fantastic on the sidewalks of New York.

TRIVIA II

by Mark Stoll

A while ago, I wrote a paper about trivia. It was mainly technical trivia. When I got done writing it, I promised that I would write one about the entertainment industry. So, here it is:

Peter Frampton got his start in a band known as Humble Pie. In fact, Peter Frampton formed the band Humble Pie. Eventually, though, he left the band, citing creative differences as the reason for his departure. He struck out on his own, in search of a solo career. It was a good move for him, as he had phenomenal success with his album Frampton Comes Alive. In fact, it sold 17 million copies, making it the best selling album to that date. That spot was previously held by Carole King's Tapestry album, which had sold 14 million copies. But his career success was soon hampered when he got into a bad automobile accident while touring the Bahamas. By the time he recovered from the accident, it was too late, as he had lost most of his career momentum. Despite his best efforts, he never managed to gain much of that momentum back.

There was once a band called the Small Faces. Why was that their name? It is because all of the band members were less than five and a half feet tall. Eventually, they changed their name to the Faces. After the band broke up, one of the band members continued to perform. You know him simply as Rod Stewart.

Huey Lewis and the News were at one time called Huey Lewis and the American Express. However, the company of the same name that issues credit cards didn't like it, so they made the band change their name. Also, at one time, their front man was a band member other than Huey Lewis. However, one day, Huey Lewis was singing along to the music, and the band decided that they like his voice better than the lead singer's voice. So, the band made those two switch places. And that is how he got a job as front man for the band.

There is another band that also went through some personnel changes. You know them as Van Halen. When they first started out, Eddy Van Halen was actually the drummer, and his brother Alex Van Halen was actually the guitar player. But it soon became apparent that Eddy was a better guitar player, and Alex was a better drummer. So, they decided to trade places. That was a good move, as it greatly improved their sound.

Gibson designed a guitar called the Flying V guitar. It has a distinctive mod shape like no other guitar. Basically, it is a three-sided guitar with straight lines rather than curves and contours making up the body. It was designed that way because some people were complaining that they don't like the shape of ordinary guitars. The problem is that you cannot lean an ordinary guitar up against a wall without it falling over. You have to have a guitar stand to hold it up. So, the Flying V was invented. When leaned against a wall, the body looks like an upside down V, thereby giving it "legs" to stand on. If you want to see what one looks like, just look at the front cover of the Allied Forces album by the Canadian rock group Triumph.

Country singer Travis Tritt is a republican, which is somewhat unusual for a celebrity. But also, he is a drag racer. He tries to schedule his concerts at places that are near drag strips. That way, he can drag race in the day, and perform on stage at night nearby. Such was the case a few years ago when I saw him at National Trail Raceway near Columbus one day, and then saw him again that night performing at Polaris Amphitheater, just outside Columbus. By the way, just in case you were wondering, he drives a Pontiac, and he ran a quarter mile in 14 seconds. Way to go, Travis!

Why is George Jones called the Possum? It is because years ago, he went into a recording studio to cut an album. The man at the front desk did not know his name. He took one look at his face, and then he told the manager that a possum has showed up to meet with him. The name stuck. So, ever since then, George Jones has been known as the Possum.

A bad thing can actually turn out to be a mixed blessing. As an example, years go, there was a man who was a schoolteacher. One of his students was a big girl, and she was rather upset about a poor grade that she received in that class. She decided to go do something about it. So, she slugged him in the face nice and hard. That inspired him to go home and write a song about it. It turned out to be a big hit song or him. What was the title of that song, and who was that man? I'll put it this way: You don't mess around with Jim. Yes, I am talking about Jim Croce.

Where did the rock group REO Speedwagon get their name? They got it from a fire truck that was made in Lansing, Michigan. The group's front man is Kevin Cronin. When he was young, he was taking guitar lessons. He would ride his bike to his guitar teacher's house. There were bullies in the neighborhood, and they would torture him. They would knock him off his bike, grab his guitar, and smash it. He would tell his mom and dad about it, but they told him not to retaliate, because what goes around comes round, just like bad Karma. After he started to get good at playing guitar, all the girls started hanging around him. Then, all the bullies started hanging around him and acting like they were his friends, because they figured it would be a good excuse to be at the right place at the right time and meet some of those girls. Then, one night, Kevin was at dance party. There was a nice looking girl standing across the room, and she started walking over towards him. All the bullies were excited, because they figured that perhaps that nice looking girl was coming over to talk to them. But instead, she walked right past them without even looking at them, and asked Kevin to dance. That inspired Kevin to go home later on and write the song, "She Doesn't Like the Tough Guys". Way to go, Kevin!

Jimi Hendrix was quite a showman. He used to smash guitars on stage. He used to pour lighter fluid on them and set them on fire. His dad owned a house in Sussex, England. But after his dad passed away, all the surviving family members were cleaning up the house and were getting ready to sell it. When they were cleaning out the garage, they found something behind a stack of old boxes. What was it? It was a guitar that had been set on fire. In fact, it was concluded that it was the same guitar that Jimi set on fire at the Isle of Wight concert. So, they put it in an auction online to see what it would fetch. It ended up selling for about 350,000 English Pounds, which is equivalent to about 500,000 American Dollars. That's a nice chunk of change. Jimi, you're the man!

There is a southern rock group that would hold band practice in a band member's basement. The old man who lived next door didn't like it a bit, because he thought it was just noise. After a while, it started to get to him. Eventually, he could take it no longer. So, he decided to go over there and do something about it. He kicked the basement window in, pointed a gun in through the window, and aimed it at the lead singer's head. He started screaming threats and obscenities at him. What was the name of the band, and what kind of a gun was it? It was a .38 Special, and now you know how that band got their name.

Well, that's my trivia paper on the entertainment industry. I hope you enjoyed it. Peace.

Biographies

Susan C. Barto

Born 6/21/41. Parents Eda and William Forcellon. Spouse: Harry W. Barto. Children: William M. Barto. Education: Katherine Gibbs School, Union College, New Jersey, Seton Hall, New Jersey. Extensive travel: Egypt, France, Italy, and England. Occupation: Legal Secretary, Legislative Aide, Writer last 20 years. Memberships: Past President Friends of the Hunterdon Museum of Art, Director of Volunteers at the Hunterdon Museum of Art, New Providence Library Board, New Providence, New Jersey, Raritan Valley College Book Group. Honors: Gold-en Certificate Awards, Drury Publishing, Plaque of Appreciation from the New Providence Library Board, Listed in Who's Who in America 1999/2000 Who's Who in the East and 2000 Who's Who in America. Have been listed in numerous Who's Who's for all 68 the past years since 2000 including 2007. Personal note: Married for 41 years to husband, Harry, who died in 2001. One son, William, who died in 2000. I love to write. Writing defines who I am.

Publishing Credits: Thirteen stories published by Creative With Words, 2 stories published by Writer's Guidelines and News. One story published in Yesterday's Magazette, One story published in a Reminisce hard cover book "The Fabulous Fifties", 3 stories published in Reminisce Magazine, and two stories published in Good Old Days Magazine. Many stories in Drury anthologies and seven books of stories published by Drury Publishing.

Palm Sunday is a saga about an Italian American family growing up in Brooklyn. The story follows the adventures of this large warm family as they move from Brooklyn to New Jersey and some as far as Florida. However, no matter how far the family is flung from each other they gather each Palm Sunday and Christmas to celebrate the holiday and more importantly the family. The story centers on five female cousins and how they grow and prosper-their loves, joys and sorrows. The story moves between the present time and the past telling of their parents and grandparents and how the family came to this country. The story concerns the grandparents and parents and their lives and fortunes and the children who in turn grow to have children and even grandchildren of their own. Each Palm Sunday and Christmas the family members reconnect and join together sharing their lives.

born and raised in Pittsburgh, PA, lives there still with her husband of fifty-four years, Nick Mother, grandmother and great grandmother, now retired, spends much of her time reading and studying her Bible, working on her writing, which she has been involved in now for nineteen years. She writes poetry and short stories and loves the small press magazines from across the country which give her a chance to have her work published for which she is most grateful Having no formal education other than her GE.D. for a high school diploma, she believes whatever talent she may have has been given to her as a gift from her heavenly Father, to share her feelings which may in some way, be just what someone would like or need to hear. She hopes her writings express her passion for life, her love and devotion to God, family and country. All glory be to the LORD.

I'm widowed and live in the country, in north Idaho, with my handicapped son. We enjoy the life here and all the wildlife we see. I have three older offspring who are married.

I've been writing for many years, actually since I was around ten years old and have been writing steadily for the past fifteen years or so.

My interests are many and varied. I love to travel, read, write, do craft work, garden, cook, and enjoy music of many kinds.

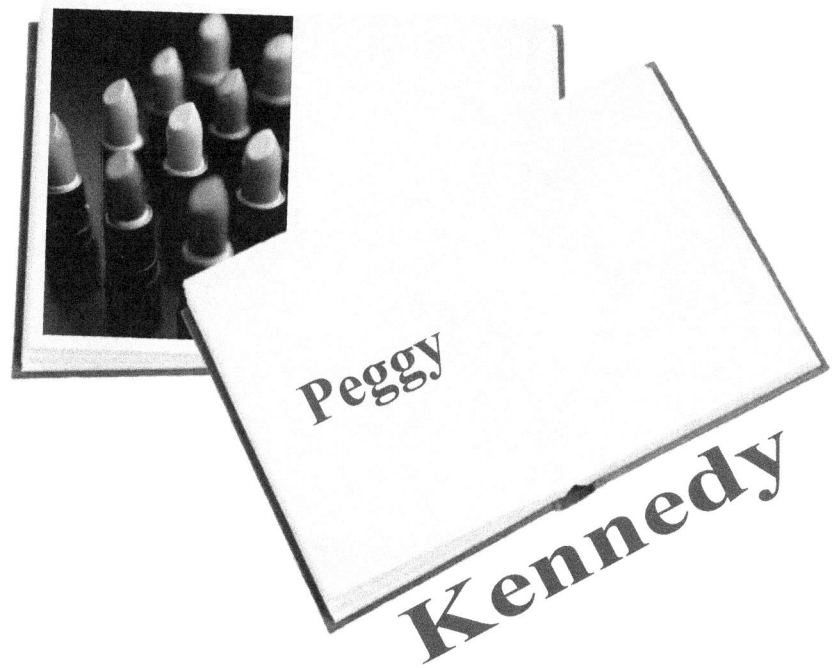

Peggy Kennedy

has published over 600 poems, six stories, one short short
story, and one essay. She is currently published in Gary
Drury Publishing anthologies and the Drury Gazette and
Inside Passages, the last published in Ketchikan, AK.
where she currently resides.

She has been published for forty five years. She is currently working on a novel, Wolf's MOON. She practices green
daily. She has been listed in WHO'S WHO IN POETRY
for fifteen years.

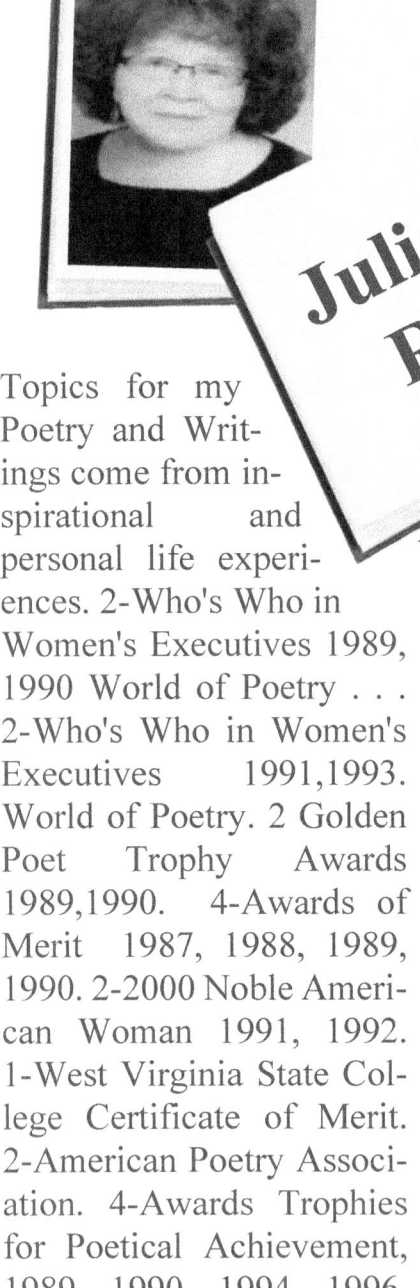

Topics for my Poetry and Writings come from inspirational and personal life experiences. 2-Who's Who in Women's Executives 1989, 1990 World of Poetry . . . 2-Who's Who in Women's Executives 1991,1993. World of Poetry. 2 Golden Poet Trophy Awards 1989,1990. 4-Awards of Merit 1987, 1988, 1989, 1990. 2-2000 Noble American Woman 1991, 1992. 1-West Virginia State College Certificate of Merit. 2-American Poetry Association. 4-Awards Trophies for Poetical Achievement, 1989, 1990, 1994, 1996.

The American Poetry Association has printed some of her works in the following Anthology Treasure Books. American Poetry Anthology 1987 and 1990. Best New Poets 1989 and 1990. Loves Greatest Treasures 1988. The World of Poetry has printed some of her Poetry in the following Anthologies. Great Poems of the Western World. World of Poetry 1989 and 1990. World of Poetry 1989 and 1990. World Treasury of Golden Poems. Mrs Lynch has received listings in publications as follows: Anthology listing 2000 NOTABLE AMERICAN WOMEN. Who's Who World Wide Platinum 1992. Professional Societies, The American Biographical Association, The International Platform Association, 25 Year Member of the Charleston Woman's Club, 36 Year Member of the Clendenin Woman's Club, American Biographical Inner Circle, Who's Who World Wide Platinum 1993, West Virginia Writer's Inc., The National Library of Poetry, Golden Rod Conference of Writer's, Clendenin Public Library Board, Clendenin's Writer's Group. Publication by the Author: Joy In The Morning, Book of Written Poetry, Writings and Reading's for Community Affairs, Flames of Mame historical novel Drury's Publications . . . Anthologies and Publications of Poetry and Writings, The Clendenin Herald Newspaper and The Clendenin Town and Country Newspaper, The Country Times Newspaper, Certificate from Gary Drury Publisher Writer Laureate for Juliet Rhodes Lynch.

My goal since 1979 has been to have something in the mail every Friday. It works. I've had over 5,000 stories, articles and poems published in textbooks, anthologies and magazines. Fourteen collections of my poems have also been published. My poems have been used on TV, CD's, audio tapes for the blind, in Braille, on PBS radio and in mail art shows including a show in Osaka, Japan.

Born:05/11/37. **Parents:** Paul and Vera Shvedchikov.
Spouse: Nina Shvedchikov. **Children:** Not. Education:
Graduate Moscow State University, Russia, 1960. Occupation: Chief of Chemistry, Pulsation Technology Corporation, Los Angels, CA. Memberships: International
Society of Poets, World Congress of Poets, International
Association of Writers and Artists. He published more
than 150 scientific papers and about 300 of his poems in
different International Magazines and Anthologies. His
poems translated into Italian, German, Spanish, Portuguese, Greek, Chinese, Japanese, and Hindi languages.

I have lived in Columbus since 1988, and I am an Ohio native. I started writing poetry in 1994. My other hobbies include camping, biking, reading, and photography, to name a few. I have an associate degree in electronics from Columbus State Community College. I currently work for an electrician's shop on the north side of Columbus. We design and build circuit boards from the ground up.

Marian H. Youngquist

was born and raised in Salem, Oregon. Throughout her ninety years she has written for newspapers, magazines and won prizes for plays and poetry. After three novels— *Procula*, *The Rocky Road Year*, *A String of Pearls*, and a memoir (private), she is at work on a fourth novel. She also lectures on Roman history. She and her husband Ted, a retired Lutheran minister, live in Wauwatosa, WI. They have four children, six grandchildren, and four great granddaughters.

Born: September 24, 1927, Archer, Florida, lived also, total of 30 years in Kansas City, Kansas; Chattanooga, Tennessee; Louisville, Kentucky, and Detroit, Michigan. It was in Louisville when I began writing songs and poetry around 1977, Basically writing of my life. I have lived every one of them. They are about people who have touched my life in a special way, nature, my pets, love, spiritual. God has been my soul teacher and mentor. Numerous awards. I leave my works to bear witness to Christ Jesus. **Parents:** Zofia and John Gocek. **Spouse:** Charles R. Walden. **Children:** Lisa Maria Walden.

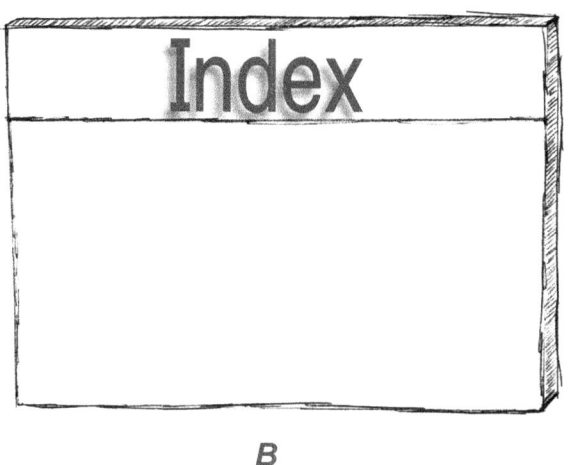

Index

www.ingramcontent.com/pod-product-compliance
Lightning Source LLC
Chambersburg PA
CBHW071347130626

46556CB00005B/2073